For Terry, Katherine, Matt, Becca, and Jackson, and all of my book-loving family—S. L. G.

For Teresa, who always helps me out whenever I'm stuck—J. W.

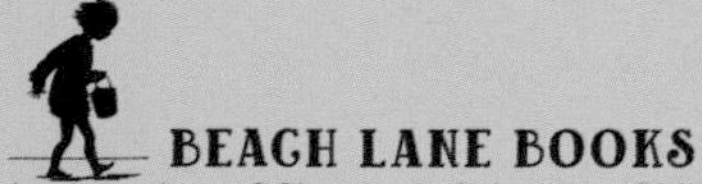

BEACH LANE BOOKS
An imprint of Simon & Schuster Children's Publishing Division • 1230 Avenue of the Americas, New York, New York 10020 • • For information about special discounts for bulk purchases, please contact Simon & Schuster Special Sales at 1-866-506-1949 or business@simonandschuster.com. • The Simon & Schuster Speakers Bureau can bring authors to your live event. For more information or to book an event, contact the Simon & Schuster Speakers Bureau at 1-866-248-3049 or visit our website at www.simonspeakers.com. • Book design by Lauren Rille • The text for this book is set in Baker Street. • The illustrations for this book are rendered in pencil and then colored digitally.
Manufactured in China
0716 SCP
First Edition
10 9 8 7 6 5 4 3 2 1
Library of Congress Cataloging-in-Publication Data
Gallion, Sue Lowell.
Pug meets Pig / Sue Lowell Gallion ; illustrated by Joyce Wan.—First edition.
p. cm.
Summary: Pug is happy at home until Pig arrives, when he must share his bowl, his yard, and even his bed, but just as Pug is packing his belongings to leave, things change for the better.
ISBN 978-1-4814-2066-2 (hardcover : alk. paper)
ISBN 978-1-4814-2067-9 (eBook)
[1. Pigs—Fiction. 2. Pug—Fiction. 3. Dogs—Fiction.] I. Wan, Joyce, illustrator. II. Title.
PZ7.1.G348Pug 2016
[E]—dc23
2015005170

written by

Sue Lowell Gallion

PUG MEETS PIG

PUG

illustrated by

Joyce Wan

Beach Lane Books • New York London Toronto Sydney New Delhi

This is Pug's home.
This is where Pug lives.

This is Pug's bowl.
This is where Pug eats.

This is Pug's yard.
This is where Pug works.

And this is Pug's bed.
This is where Pug sleeps.

Pug is happy here at home,
with his bowl, his yard, and his bed.

But one day when the door opens . . .

out trots someone new.

Pig meets Pug.

Pug meets Pig.

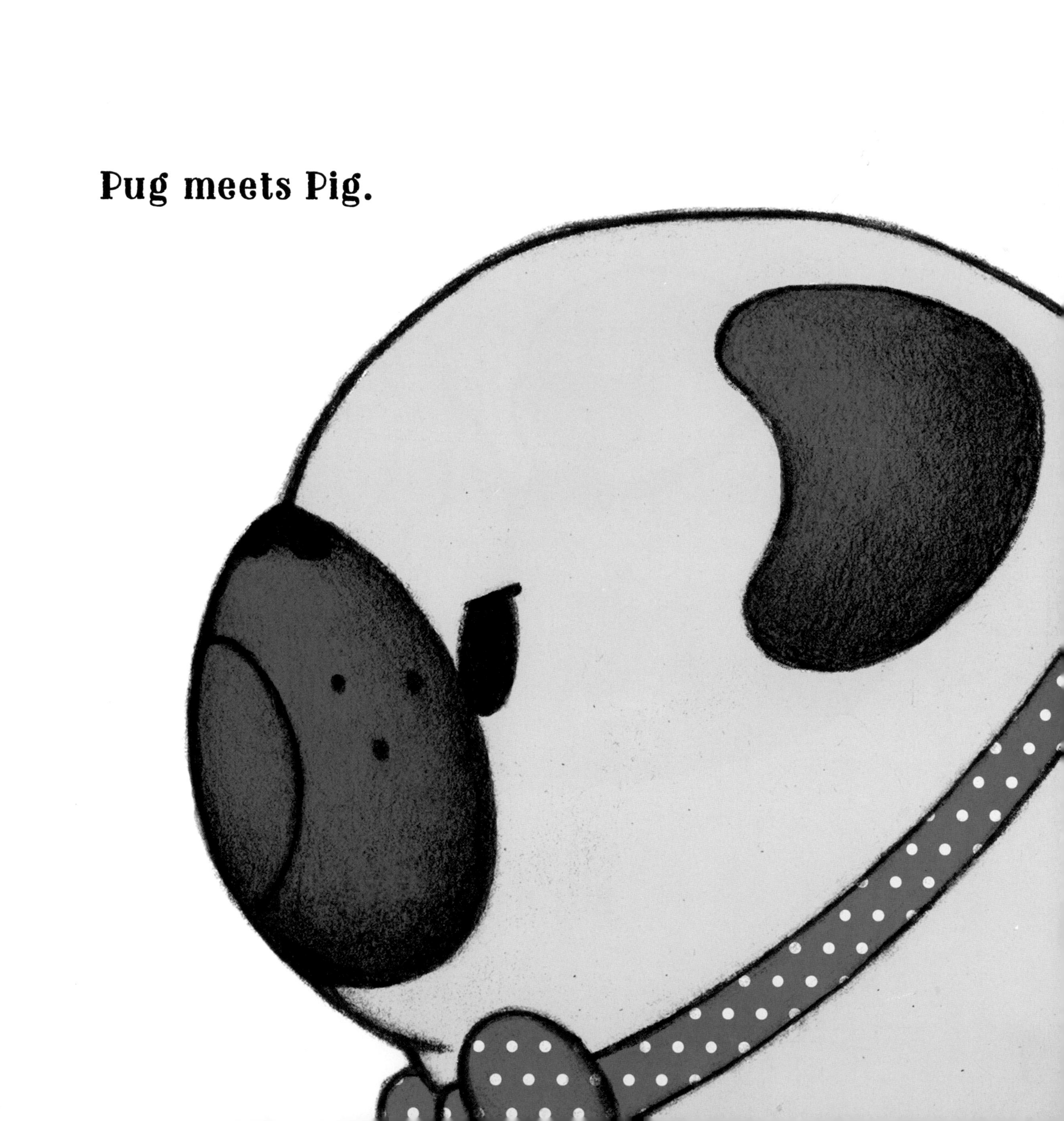

Pug is hungry.

But here is Pig.

Pug has work to do.

But here is Pig.

Pug needs some sleep.

But here is Pig!

Pug is not happy.
He is not happy here at home anymore.

Pug cannot stay here.

He packs his things.

But wait!
What’s this?
PUG

Now Pug can
come and go
without Pig!

Once again,
Pug is happy here at home.

But someone else is not . . .

Pig's head can fit
through the doggy door.

Pig's tail can fit
through the doggy door.

But Pig's round middle cannot fit.

What a sad Pig!

Perhaps Pug could help.

Perhaps Pug should help.

Perhaps Pug *will* help.

Pug scratches and gnaws.
He chews and claws.
And then the doggy
door for Pug . . .

is also a piggy door for Pig!

Now this is where Pug and Pig eat.

This is where Pug and Pig work.

This is where Pug and Pig sleep.

Pug is happy here at home . . .

and so is Pig.